Wilting of Winter and Worry

Verses of Decay, Doubt, and the Dimming Light

Edgar J. Wilde

"I carry the silence of snow in my chest,
a hush so heavy it forgets how to melt."

Copyright Page

Wilting of Winter and Worry
Verses of Decay, Doubt, and the Dimming Light

First Edition: February 2026
ISBN: 979-8-9921931-5-2

Published by Bell of Ash And Sky Press

For permissions or inquiries, contact:

Edgar J. Wilde

Edgarjwilde@gmail.com

Dedication

As always, for the one – who knows who they are. You were my muse, my ache, my hope…..now, you are simply mine.

For you, Ashley, those three words…… I LOVE YOU.

Acknowledgments

For my parents, grandparents and those who have supported me through the emotions expressed in this book.

My muse. Who inspires the emotions and feelings that become the words for most of the writings in this book. You are the source of all the happy and positive, whereas my inability to manage being without you, is the source of the negative. You bring nothing but light whereas I am the bringer of the dark. Now, you bring me everything and the love we have is unmatched.

To those who read this, I hope the words can resonate with you, offer solace, or simply remind you that you're not alone in your own journey.

To MB, (Boss), thank you for your support, encouragement, and for never judging. May you rest peacefully, taken too soon.

- **Edgar**

"The cracks weren't flaws – they were the only way the light ever got in."

Content Advisory

I usually don't subscribe to the idea of "trigger warnings," as I believe there's value in facing what makes us feel or react. Each encounter, uncomfortable as it may be, can help us build resilience. Shielding ourselves from discomfort can sometimes dull our capacity to cope, potentially doing more harm than good. That said, I am neither a doctor nor a psychiatrist, and I respect that everyone's journey is unique.

This collection explores themes of self-harm, suicide, love and loss, heartbreak, addiction, and self-worth. These poems aren't crafted for shock; they are simply reflections of my own feelings and experiences. I hope you'll continue to read, as growth often comes from stepping beyond the familiar and exploring what lies beyond our comfort zones.

Thank you for walking with me through these pages.

Opening Note

This is not a tidy book.

Like the other books in this series, I wrote most of it while drunk. Or worse. Or both. There were nights I bled onto the page with a bottle in one hand and a balloon in the other, shrooms crawling under my skin, trying to turn the chaos into something that made sense. I don't glorify it. I barely even remember parts of it. But I know I needed to write to stay alive. These poems are stitched from blackout hours and withdrawal mornings, from panic, from loneliness, from the kind of ache that makes you reach for anything just to feel different. I'm clean now. Still healing. Still here. But this book is a record of the storm I barely walked out of – and every word is proof I did.

It does not resolve itself with easy metaphors or heal within the confines of a single page. It bleeds slowly. It confesses in fragments. It remembers what it should have forgotten and forgets what it tried too hard to hold. These poems were written through quiet collapses and sacred reckonings, in the hush of night and the noise of longing. They are not about closure. They are about the truth that remains when everything else has been stripped away.

Opening Note

If you find yourself in these pages, know that you are not alone. You never were. There is no map for heartbreak, no formula for staying whole. But there is language. And sometimes, that is enough.

Never give up, through five books and many lonely nights of longing and hoping, the muse of these writings, I am happy to say, has since shared her love for me and we are together. With plans to marry in the future and continue our journey through life together.

Introduction

This collection is a journey through the tender, tangled roots of love, longing, and loss.
It begins with emptiness, descends into desire and despair, and rises, though not always triumphantly, into resilience and revelation.
These poems are not meant to offer answers. They are offerings themselves: moments captured, pain named, desire acknowledged, and strength honored. Whether whispered in grief or gasped in surrender, each piece lives in the space between breath and breaking.

Let this book be a mirror for your ache, a compass for your want, and a hand to hold in the dark.

Contents

Section I – The Ache Of Absence

"Where love used to live, silence now sleeps with the door open."

This section carries the weight of absence, the kind that doesn't always come from someone leaving, but from someone no longer showing up. It's the echo left behind when a once-familiar laugh no longer fills the room, or the way a name can still taste like longing on the tongue.

These poems are shaped by loss, but not only the loud, clean kind. They speak of slow disappearances, of emotional erosion, and of the moments when love stays in the bones long after it's left the bed. They are quiet testaments to the endurance of memory and the ache of what almost was.

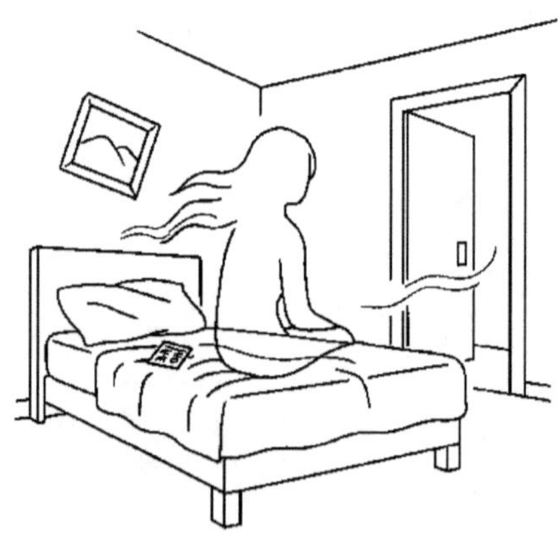

Section I – The Ache of Absence

The Place We Become Ordinary and Infinite

I don't need grand declarations,
or the weight of the world rewritten in our name.
I just want to exist with you—
in the quiet places where love lingers
long after the words have left us.
I want to wake before the sun,
not for duty, not for necessity,
but for the simple act of watching you sleep.
To memorize the curve of your breath,
the way your lashes tremble in dreams,
the way the morning light hesitates,
as if unsure whether it's worthy to touch you.
I want to stand beside you in the kitchen,
not speaking, not needing to,
passing you the coffee before you ask,
watching the steam curl into the air like
the ghost of something sacred.
Your fingers brushing mine, barely a whisper,

but enough to anchor me.

Enough to remind me that love is not the storm,

but the shelter we build inside it.

I want to know the weight of your silences,

to understand the spaces between your thoughts,

the ones you don't know how to name.

I'll hold them with care,

trace their edges with my fingertips,

and remind you they are safe here,

that I am safe here.

I want to carry the smallest pieces of you,

the scent of your hair in the cold,

the way you hum to yourself when you think no one is listening,

the half-smile you give when you're lost in thought,

the way your hand lingers just a second longer

when you reach for mine.

I want to exist with you in the moments

that slip through time unnoticed by the world.

Not just in the nights wrapped in passion,

but in the grocery store aisles,
choosing between two brands of coffee.
In the car, driving nowhere,
your hand on my leg, your voice in my ears,
your presence filling every space
I once thought would remain empty.
I want to be the place you exhale.
The quiet after a long day,
the warmth in the cold,
the thing you reach for
without thinking, without question,
because you know,
I will always be there.
Not just in the highs, not just in the moments
that glitter and shine,
but in the ordinary,
the simple,
the beautifully mundane.
I don't need anything more than this.
Than you.

Than us.

Existing, together.

Section I – The Ache of Absence

The Smile That Split the Darkness

You sat before me, shoulders curled inward,

as if trying to fold yourself into something smaller,

something easier to carry,

something that didn't take up so much space in the world.

Your voice,

a threadbare whisper unraveling at the edges,

tangled in the weight of your own self-loathing.

"I'm pathetic," you said,

as if the syllables themselves burned your tongue.

But I saw you.

Not the version you tried to hide,

not the sum of your regrets or the ache in your voice,

but you,

whole, raw, breathtaking in your ruin.

I lifted your chin,

let my gaze hold you the way the sky holds the stars,

not as something broken,

but as something burning,

something vast, something infinite.

And when I said, **"You are beautiful,"**

not despite your flaws,

not in ignorance of them,

but because of them,

because of the way they made you real,

you hesitated.

For the briefest moment,

through the sorrow swimming in your eyes,

I saw it,

the flicker of belief,

the way my words touched something in you

that had long been abandoned.

And when your lips parted,

the smallest curve of a smile forming

like dawn breaking through the thickest of nights,

I knew.

I knew my purpose was not to pull you from the darkness,

but to stand in it with you,

to trace the constellations in your scars,

to whisper love into the spaces

where you had only ever planted doubt.

To remind you, over and over,

until the words became the marrow of your bones,

you are perfectly imperfect,

and I will spend every breath

loving you deeper than love has ever known.

Section I – The Ache of Absence

The Quiet Art of a Woman Who Doesn't Know She's a Masterpiece

I have always thought you beautiful,

at first, in the way light lingers on your skin,

how it curves along the quiet slope of your cheek,

the soft defiance of your jaw,

the elegance of your slender neck,

the way your hair spills like ink against the world.

But beauty is not just what is seen.

I learned you,

unraveled the stories beneath your skin,

traced the echoes of battles fought in silence,

felt the weight of everything you carry

and the kindness you still choose to give.

And then, somehow, you became even more,

not just in the way you move through the world,

but in the way you make it feel different.

You are the pause between heartbeats,

the hush before something profound,

the shift in the air before the first note of a song
that will never leave you the same.
And you,
you do not see the beauty in the things I adore.
Your hands, delicate and uncertain,
as if they were not made to hold worlds.
And yet, they do.
They have held grief and tenderness alike,
have shaped comfort from silence,
have touched me without ever needing to reach.
Your profile, the quiet art of it,
the curve of your expression
when you think no one is watching,
I watch.
And I see something breathtaking.
So when I tell you that you are beautiful,
know that it is not just for what my eyes see,
but for what I feel when I stand near you.
For the way my pulse forgets its rhythm,
for the way existence itself feels lighter

simply because you are in it.

It is everything you are,

everything you have been,

everything you will be.

And nothing,

not time, not distance, not even doubt,

will ever make me see you

as anything less than extraordinary

Section I – The Ache of Absence

Choosing Stillness When the Storm Won't End

I wonder if the air will simply swallow the space I leave behind,

like a body rolling over in sleep,

making room for something else.

I have come to understand that life is not sacred.

It is not stitched with meaning,

not carved with purpose,

just a flickering inconvenience,

a breath taken out of obligation,

a heart that keeps beating

only because it hasn't been given a reason to stop.

They call it tragedy.

They call it sickness.

They dress it up in words like despair and hopelessness

as if sadness is an affliction,

as if it is something foreign,

something unnatural,

instead of the quiet hum
that has lived in my bones since before I had a name.
But tell me,
what is so horrific about stepping off the edge
when the fall is inevitable?
When the ground is always waiting,
patient, open-palmed,
a cradle of stone and silence?
No one mourns the wave that folds into the sea,
no one begs the autumn leaves to cling to the branch,
yet here, in this skin,
there is expectation,
to stay, to endure, to pretend the fire still warms
when all that's left is smoke.
They speak of death like it is a thief,
like it is some shadowed thing
that creeps in the night and steals what is precious,
but I do not see the horror in it.
I do not see the theft in surrender.
What is so wrong with slipping beneath the tide,

with letting the weight of all this wasted air

carry me down into the quiet?

Why is it brave to endure,

but cowardly to choose?

Why do they beg me to stay

when they do not care how much it costs me?

I am tired of paying.

Tired of carrying this body,

this rusted machine

clogged with grief and the soft rot of wasted years,

the way a fruit spoils from the inside first,

sweetness giving way to decay,

hidden beneath an unbroken skin.

Maybe the real horror

isn't the leaving.

Maybe it's the staying.

Maybe it's the sound of my own breath,

dragging in, dragging out,

a useless metronome marking time

that doesn't belong to me.

And maybe that's all I need to know.

Maybe that's the softest truth of all.

That nothing is waiting,

nothing is watching,

nothing is asking me to stay.

And I just don't want to be here anymore.

Section I – The Ache of Absence

The Side of the Bed That Became a Grave

I sleep on the edge now.

This bed, once a kingdom,

is nothing more than a single exile.

I do not turn to your side.

I do not dare.

To do so would be admitting you're not coming back.

And I can't.

Because some nights, if I close my eyes just right,

if I breathe in slow enough,

the scent of you still lingers in the pillow,

faint, like a whisper in another room,

like the ghost of a perfume bottle long tipped over.

If I press my face against the sheets,

I swear I can almost find you there.

The best sleep I ever had was the kind I never closed my eyes for.

Lying awake, arms wrapped around you,

watching the way the night curled itself around your body,

how even the moonlight softened when it touched you.

God, you looked so peaceful.

Like love had never hurt you.

Like the world had only ever been kind.

And I wanted to keep it that way.

So I held you.

I watched the rise and fall of your breath,

counted each inhale like a prayer I was too afraid to say out loud.

Even in sleep, you knew me.

I would find your hand in the dark,

and without stirring, your fingers would open,

welcoming mine like they belonged there.

Like I belonged there.

But now,

Now I lay in this silence,

listening to the absence of your breath,

the cruel stillness of air that does not move for you.

Section I – The Ache of Absence

This bed, this vast, empty bed,

has become a graveyard of touch.

And I do not turn to your side.

I do not dare.

Because if I do,

if I stretch out my hand and find nothing but cold sheets,

if I wake to the truth I already know,

it will shatter me.

And I don't think I'll survive it.

Section I – The Ache of Absence

Like the Ocean Doesn't Remember Drowning Me

It happens every time.

Like an old wound that should have healed,

but never did.

Like a ghost pressing its hand against my ribs,

whispering, you are not alone, but you are not whole either.

When I see you,

it is not just you I see.

It is every version of you I have ever known

The one who laughed at midnight with whiskey-warm lips

the one who whispered secrets into my collarbone,

the one who curled up in silence, fighting sleep,

but let herself fall anyway,

because for a moment, she felt safe.

When I see you,

my body betrays me.

My chest tightens as if my ribs have forgotten

how to do anything but hold the shape of your absence.

My pulse turns frantic,

like a trapped bird battering itself against my bones,

desperate to escape,

desperate to stay.

I feel lightheaded,

because you are oxygen

and I have spent too long trying to breathe without you.

I feel heavy,

because you are gravity

and I am the tide, pulled toward you,

even when I know I shouldn't be.

My hands shake,

as if they remember what it was like to hold you,

as if they miss the weight of your skin in my palms,

the way you used to press your fingers into mine

like you were afraid I might disappear

if you didn't grip tight enough.

Section I – The Ache of Absence

But I never disappeared.

I am still here.

I have always been here.

When I see you,

I see the words I wrote to you,

folded neatly into corners of time,

unread, unopened,

but still waiting.

I see the space you carved into my life

and the shape you left behind.

I see the moments when you let yourself feel

before you convinced yourself you shouldn't.

Before you turned away.

And yet, you smile.

And yet, you say hi.

Like the ocean doesn't remember drowning me.

Like I don't remember how to swim,

but still wade into the water,

because something in me believes

it is better to drown in you

than to never feel you at all.

So yes,

my heart races.

My body shakes.

My breath stumbles over itself,

unsure whether to leave or to stay.

Because when I see you,

I don't just see you.

I see us.

I see everything.

And maybe that is the most beautiful pain of all.

Section I – The Ache of Absence

All That I Am, All That I Will Ever Be

They rose from the dark, spined and woven,

a tangled breath of pulsing tendrils,

not quite living, not quite dead,

but something beyond, something waiting.

They did not speak in words,

but in knowing, in the weight of something vast

pressing into the hollow of my ribs.

Are you ready?

And I nodded, because I have always surrendered,

because I have never clung to this world

with anything but weary hands,

because I have stood at the edge before

and wondered how it might feel

to unmake myself.

But then,

her name rose in me like a sunrise,

a burning that split the black,

a warmth so absolute

it rewrote every shadow.

Ashley.

And suddenly, I was terrified.

Not of dying,

not of whatever waited beyond,

but of leaving before I held her again.

Before I buried my face in the soft curve of her neck

and breathed her in like the first breath after drowning.

Before I felt her fingertips skim my skin,

familiar as the lines in my palms,

as if she had traced them into being

before I was ever born.

I ached with it,

with the unbearable weight of her absence,

with the way my chest cracked open,

not from fear,

but from love so deep,

so all-consuming,

it had nowhere left to go but out,

bursting through skin and bone and soul.

I wanted her.

Not in the way the body wants,

not just in fire and hunger,

but in the way that life itself wants—

desperate, essential, irrevocable.

She is the thread that stitches me together,

the gravity that holds my orbit,

the only name I will ever whisper

into the quiet between heartbeats.

I see her in everything—

in the way light bends through my tears,

fracturing into every color she has ever made me feel.

In the way my hands tremble,

not with fear,

but with the unbearable need

to trace the constellations of freckles on her skin,

to commit them to memory,

so that if I ever lost my way,

I could navigate my way home by her alone.

Section I – The Ache of Absence

If there is a god,

they are her laughter.

If there is a heaven,

it is her arms around me.

If there is anything in this world worth clinging to,

it is the sound of her saying my name.

So no,

I am not ready.

Because she is not in that darkness.

She is here.

And for as long as she is here,

so am I

Section I – The Ache of Absence

No Legacy to Leave

They talk about words like tombstones,

stories etched into time,

books stacked like bones in the quiet corners of history—

proof that someone was here.

But who will dig through the dust when I am gone?

Who will crack the spine of my name,

trace their fingers over the ink of my thoughts

and wonder who I was?

No children to whisper my memory,

no bloodline to carry my voice in their marrow.

When the ground takes me,

it will take everything,

my words, my weight, my wanting.

No hands to find me.

No eyes to read me.

No name to call me back.

And yet,

Section I – The Ache of Absence

Let the pages yellow.

Let the ink fade.

Let time swallow me whole.

I wrote for the fire inside me,

not for the ones who come after.

I don't need a legacy.

I just needed to feel alive.

Section I – The Ache of Absence

I Will Stand Between You and the Sky

The wind will come,
pulling at the edges of the world,
whispering its restless hunger through the trees.
The sky will tighten,
folding itself into the dark hands of the storm,
thunder pressing its voice against the earth.
I know,
the air thickens before the breaking,
the silence stretches too thin,
and in that waiting, fear takes root.
But listen,
not all things bend to the storm.
There is a place where the winds unravel,
where rain softens against steady hands,
where the walls do not shake,
where the night does not reach.
And you,

you will never have to stand alone beneath the weight of the sky.

If the storm calls your name,

I will stand between you and the thunder,

open my hands to the lightning,

take the rain so it never touches your skin.

And if the winds should ever pull too strong,

if the ground beneath you turns to water,

I will cross the flood,

step into the howl of the storm,

walk through the unrelenting dark,

just to bring you home.

Because there is no sky I would not defy,

no distance I would not travel,

no force strong enough to keep me from where you stand.

You will always have a place where the storm breaks.

You will always have shelter here

Section I – The Ache of Absence

The Weight of What Remains

I live on scraps of you,

small mercies that never fill me,

but keep me just alive enough to feel hunger.

A half-breathed word, a glance too long,

the ghost of your handprint on a doorframe

I still trace when no one is watching.

I have trained myself to survive on less,

on fragments of a life I no longer belong to,

on the way you let my name slip

only when the world is soft with drink.

A whispered confession you'll wake and forget,

but I gather it like rain in a desert,

tilting my mouth toward the sky

for even the smallest drop.

And still, you keep them.

The first bouquet I ever gave you,

its stems brittle now, its colors faded,

its petals fallen like relics of something sacred,

and you, you did not sweep them away,
did not let them scatter into nothing.
You collected them.
Placed them in the vase alongside what was left,
as if even in their death, they still meant something.
As if even the broken pieces were worth keeping.
I don't know what that means.
If I am still there, if I am a ghost in your home
the way you are a ghost in me.
If those petals are a kindness or a cruelty,
if they are proof of a love that lingers
or just the habit of holding onto what once was.
I tell myself it means something.
I have to.
Because I am starving,
and hope is the only thing I can still swallow.

Section I – The Ache of Absence

How to Drown Without Making a Sound

I say her name and it unspools inside me,

like thread pulled from the center of something fraying,

something breaking.

It is the only prayer I have ever known,

the only curse I will never outrun.

She is the breath that fills my lungs,

and I am drowning in her.

Every inhale is an offering,

every exhale is a plea.

She is both the air that keeps me alive

and the hand pressing against my ribs,

reminding me that I was never meant to breathe easy.

I have loved her in a way that does not save me.

Loved her like an anchor loves the ocean floor,

heavy, desperate, incapable of letting go.

She is the tide that lifts me

just high enough to see the sky,

just long enough to remember

what it felt like to believe in something like flight,

before she pulls me under again.

And I go willingly.

I let the weight of her drag me beneath,

let the current of her indifference fold around me

like a lullaby meant for the lost.

There is a kind of comfort in it,

this knowing that I will never be enough,

this ache that has carved itself into my ribs,

into the marrow of who I am.

I have called this longing by a thousand names,

love, devotion, ruin,

but they all taste the same in the end.

They all sound like a door closing

before I can reach it.

She is the reason I hold on.

The reason I keep breathing,

even when the air turns to glass in my throat.

And yet, she is the reason I want to stop.

Section I – The Ache of Absence

The reason I feel the edge pressing against my back,

the reason I stare too long into the kind of darkness

that does not offer light.

I carry her in my chest,

a stone against my sternum,

a boulder chained to my ankle.

And maybe this is what love has always been,

not a soft place to land,

but the slow sinking into something you cannot escape.

Maybe love is learning how to drown

without ever opening your mouth.

Section I – The Ache of Absence

A Love That Refuses to Die

When does it stop?

Does it ever stop?

Or is love, once awakened, a thing that refuses death,

a wound that never clots,

an ache that learns to live in the hollow spaces

where something whole used to be?

I do not beg for relief.

I do not plead for forgetting.

This pain, this quiet, endless ache, is mine.

A companion I did not choose,

but one I have made room for,

one that sleeps beside me,

breathes in time with me,

fills the silence where your voice should be.

I wear it like second skin,

a layer so tightly bound to me

that I do not know where I end

and sorrow begins.

Section I – The Ache of Absence

To tear it from me would be to unmake myself,

to strip me raw,

to leave nothing but a pulsing, gasping absence

where even suffering used to be.

And I do not want that.

I do not want the quiet.

I do not want the emptiness where you used to live.

I will carry this love,

even as it weighs heavier with time,

even as it drags behind me like a shadow

on a road with no end.

Because to stop feeling

would be the truest kind of death.

And I was yours,

even in the leaving,

even in the breaking,

even now,

even always.

Section I – The Ache of Absence

This Is How I Say It Without Saying It

It sits behind my teeth,

pressing against my tongue like a tide,

rising, relentless, aching to be set free.

I love you.

I feel it in the way my hands still reach for you,

in the way my breath still holds

when you are near,

in the silence that swells between us,

heavy with all that cannot be spoken.

I do not say it,

not because it is untrue,

not because I fear the weight of it,

but because I know what it would do to you.

Because I have seen the way your eyes soften

then go still,

the way your lips part as if to answer,

before you swallow the words back down,

bury them beneath the wreckage of what cannot be.

Section I – The Ache of Absence

I do not say it,

because I do not need to hear the absence of it

in your voice.

But I hope you feel it,

in the way I stay,

in the way my hands never let you feel alone,

in the way I turn toward you

as if pulled by something I could never fight.

I hope you feel it

in every action I take,

in every word I do not say,

in every quiet moment

where love is the only thing

that fills the space between us.

I do not say it.

But it is there.

Always.

Section I – The Ache of Absence

A Match That Was Never Struck For Me

I have held love like water in my hands,
felt it slip between my fingers,
watched it soak into the earth,
leaving nothing but dampened skin,
a memory of something that was never mine.
I have given love like fire,
burned myself to keep others warm,
left my hands raw from reaching,
from holding too tightly,
from cupping dying embers
that were never meant to last.
But to be loved,
what must it feel like?
To be something someone holds without urgency,
without fear of slipping away.
To be the warmth, not the flame.
To be the thing someone stays for,
not the thing they leave behind.

Section I – The Ache of Absence

I wonder if it is like standing in the sun,

not bracing for the cold that follows.

Or like breathing in the ocean,

without fearing the pull of the tide.

I do not know.

I only know how to be the giving hands,

the burning match,

the voice that says I am here

to an echo that never answers back.

Section I – The Ache of Absence

Fluent in a Language Never Spoken Back

I have only ever known love as something I give
Poured out from my hands like water,
pressed into the spaces between my ribs,
woven into the quiet places of others,
so they never have to feel alone.
I have given love like fire,
let it consume me,
let it strip me down to bone and open hands,
burned just to keep someone else from shivering.
And when they were warm,
they left.
Every time, they left.
But to be loved,
what must it feel like?
To be something someone stays for,
not a lesson they needed to learn.
To be chosen, without hesitation,
without an exit strategy or an expiration date.

Section I – The Ache of Absence

To be held,

not just when I am useful,

not just when I am easy to love,

but when I am heavy,

when I am too much,

when I am quiet, and shaking,

and waiting for the door to close again.

I have seen love in the way I look at others,

in the way I remember the little things,

in the way I say, I'll stay and mean it.

But I have never seen love in the way someone looks at me.

Never felt it in the spaces they carve for me in their lives,

because there are no spaces.

Only cracks too small to step into,

only arms that hold me when it is convenient,

only echoes of words that never meant what I thought they did.

And so I wonder,

is love always supposed to ache?

Section I – The Ache of Absence

Is it supposed to be a hunger with no feast?

A reaching with no landing?

A language I speak fluently,

but have never heard spoken back?

What must it feel like

to be the thing someone cannot bear to lose?

To be the arms they run to,

not the lesson they learn and leave behind?

I do not know.

I only know how to love.

How to give until I am empty,

how to offer and offer and offer

and never ask,

because I already know the answer.

I only know how to be the one who stays,

who burns,

who holds,

who watches love walk away,

without ever turning back.

Section I – The Ache of Absence

Section I – The Ache of Absence

Taste of the Decaying Sunrise and Whispers to the Forgotten God

I have become

a museum of unmade mornings.

Rotting sunrises in my throat,

each one choked down like a bitter pill

washed with whiskey spit and sleep I didn't earn.

My hands shake like prayer

but I've long forgotten the god.

So I light another offering,

let the gas hiss a lullaby,

fill the lungs like apology,

slow, blue, blooming at the edges.

I keep a shelf of escape

in amber bottles with childproof lids

they never meant to stop children like me.

Tiny soldiers,

names too long to mean anything

except maybe this time.

Section I – The Ache of Absence

I swallow alphabets
hoping for silence in a language I can't speak.
Shrooms like coins on my eyes,
buying a passage out of this skin.
Out of this room.
Out of this ache that keeps dressing itself
in my clothes and walking around
like it owns my name.
I've taken razors to the paper of my body,
drawn inkless lines that only bleed regret.
Not for attention,
but to watch the pain leave me in streams,
to prove I still exist beneath the static.
Sometimes I need to see the damage
to believe it's mine.
The drink stings less now.
It's not celebration.
It's shelter.
A quiet room where I don't have to be
anything with a future.

Section I – The Ache of Absence

I roll the dice every night,

Will I sleep

or shut off?

Will I wake

or will the black stay pulled tight like a curtain

and finally,

finally

fall?

I don't want to die.

But I don't want to keep living like this,

wearing grief like a second skin,

dragging my limbs like meat

through a world that only ever chews.

So I build a silence

from the things that dull me.

Mix chemicals like paint,

color over the sharp corners

until my mind is just a fog

where nothing grows

and nothing hurts.

Section I – The Ache of Absence

This is not poetry.

It's a fucking autopsy.

Every word

a bruise peeled open.

Every sentence

a new excuse

to not scream.

But if you're listening,

and I mean really listening,

then maybe this

is the first time

I've said

I don't want to be numb.

I just don't know how

to feel

and survive it.

Section II – The Pulse of Want

"Want is a hunger that doesn't wait for permission."

Here lies the ache that comes before the fall, the fire that dances on the edge of need. Desire, in all its forms, pulses beneath the skin: messy, consuming, insistent. This section explores the magnetic pull between bodies and hearts, the yearning that sharpens breath and stirs unrest. These aren't soft wishes whispered to the stars; they are clawing cravings that leave you breathless and undone. Want, here, is not painted as something shameful, but as something beautifully human, proof that we are still alive and still rcaching.

Section II – The Pulse of Want

Gravity in the Ruins

I wake in the ache of you,

where silence stains the air between us,

where love is not gone, only displaced,

lurking in the margins of words unsaid.

I map the distance in my ribs,

the hollowed-out places where your voice used to settle,

the echoes of your name still dragging through my blood

like a tide that never learned how to recede.

Tell me, when did we become the stor

instead of the shelter?

When did the wind turn sharp,

twisting us into strangers

who still recognize each other's hands?

I do not know how to stand in your absence,

how to name this longing when it is not griefbut something crueler,

something with teeth, something alive,

something that tightens when I try to walk away.

We have unraveled and rewoven,

burned down and rebuilt,

but always in the ashes, I find the thread,

the thin, unbreakable pulse,

pulling me back to you.

Why do we choose exile from each other

when every cell in us begs for home?

Why do we deny the inevitable,

pretend the universe did not script us into the same page,

the same breath, the same night sky?

Tell me, love, what is this punishment for?

What lesson have we not yet learne

that we must still suffer the space between us?

Or is it simply this,

that we have never been free,

that love like ours was never meant to be gentle,

only undeniable,

only written into the bones of the stars,

only waiting, waiting, waiting

for us to surrender to what we already know?

Section II – The Pulse of Want

Redacted

I am never the name etched into stone,

never the ink that stains their fingers.

Not the headline, not the front page,

just the weight of an ellipsis trailing behind someone else's thought.

I am the smudge where a name should be,

the aftertaste of a conversation no one remembers starting.

The ghost in the group photo,

present, but only in the way absence is present.

I have learned that silence is a shape you can fit inside,

that a shadow is just a body forgotten by the light.

I have mastered the art of almost,

of stepping forward only to find the floor gone.

When they write their histories,

I am a name between two commas,

a placeholder, a bridge, a breath between more important moments.

Something to be skimmed over.

If I screamed,

I think the sound would dissolve before it reached them,

a thing erased before it ever existed.

Some people live like exclamation points,

loud, certain, demanding space.

I have always been parentheses,

something that could be removed

and the sentence wouldn't notice.

I am not the headline.

Not the story.

Not the ink.

Just the empty space where something else should be.

Section II – The Pulse of Want

"Wasted Heartbeats"

I am not here,

not really,

not in any way that matters,

not in any way that leaves a mark on this world

or in the spaces where I used to belong.

I am air trapped in a collapsed lung,

a whisper swallowed before it can reach a name,

a voice echoing off walls that forgot what it means to listen.

Every breath is an execution, slow and practiced,

a blade dragged against the throat of time,

again, and again, and again.

My lungs do not expand with purpose,

they do not fill with want.

They only rise because they are told to,

because something inside me

hasn't yet received the message that I do not wish to continue.

Section II – The Pulse of Want

I exist in the spaces between replies,
a body stranded in silence,
a heart beating only for its own mockery.
What is a pulse but a death march,
a metronome ticking down the seconds
until I become a forgotten song?
I walk in a rhythm I did not choose,
marching to a drum I did not ask for,
following a path that does not want me,
toward a grave I have already carved into my bones.
Every heartbeat without you is a wasted one,
a ghost of what could have been,
a sound too hollow to hold meaning.
Every second I do not spend
replying to your voice
is another second of screaming silence,
a cavern of noise inside my skull
where your name is the only word
that ever meant anything.
And I am tired.

Section II – The Pulse of Want

Not the kind of tired that sleep can fix,

not the kind of tired that passes like a wave

or lifts like fog in the morning.

I am tired in the way that roots rot,

in the way that old wood breaks beneath the weight of time.

I am tired of opening my eyes to a world that does not open for me.

Tired of this body,

tired of this breath,

tired of the way my chest rises only to collapse again.

I want to be untethered.

Not just gone,

but never having been.

I want the past to forget me,

for the memories to unspool like frayed thread

until there is nothing left to sew back together.

I do not belong in this skin.

I do not belong in this place.

I do not belong in this life

that only exists as a shadow of the one I wanted.

And if I could,

I would fold myself into the dark,

disappear into the spaces where lost things go,

slip between the seconds like an unfinished sentence

left hanging in the air,

waiting for someone to notice that it was never meant to end.

But instead,

I breathe.

Again, and again, and again.

And I don't know why.

Maybe it's habit.

Maybe it's the way the world refuses to let go of the things

that have already let go of themselves.

Maybe it's because a small, stubborn part of me

still waits for a message,

still holds onto the hope

that one more heartbeat might be worth something,

that one more breath

might carry her name back to me.

Maybe it's nothing at all.

Maybe I am just a body

waiting to become a ghost.

And maybe that's all I have ever been.

Section II – The Pulse of Want

I Orbit What Won't Hold Me

How can you forget me

when I am tangled in the fabric of your absence,

when my thoughts orbit you endlessly,

a moon caught in the pull of a planet

that does not acknowledge its tides?

I breathe you in like a sickness,

let you settle into my lungs,

while you exhale me without noticing,

without consequence,

without ever tasting the air I've become.

I am convinced the universe must work differently than this.

That this much feeling cannot dissolve into nothing,

that the weight of my wanting must press against you,

must ripple through your skin like a shiver you cannot place,

must echo somewhere inside you,

even if you do not know its name.

But maybe I am wrong.

Section II – The Pulse of Want

Maybe love is not an energy that transfers,

maybe longing does not leave fingerprints,

maybe I am only the planet choking on what you discard,

swallowing the pieces you never meant to leave behind.

You litter me without a second thought,

and I gather every scrap,

mistaking your pollution for something precious,

holding my breath against the fumes of forgetting

while you walk away clean.

Section II – The Pulse of Want

When Empty Hands Refuse to Catch You Again

I have given you everything,
words that lifted you,
praise that steadied you,
a sanctuary built from patience
and the softness of my voice.
You came to me with hands open,
empty, expectant,
and I filled them, always.
Offered you warmth when the world was cold,
listened when no one else would.
Held space for the weight of your grief
while I carried mine alone.
But I watch you,
giving away what I've never had.
Your touch, your time, your body,
offered so freely, so cheaply,
to hands that never trembled for you,
to lips that never spoke your name with care.

Section II – The Pulse of Want

Yet I, steadfast,

have waited in the shadows of your indifference,

starving while you feast on lesser loves.

No more.

I will not be your place of rest

when you return hollowed out and empty.

I will not pour into you

when you leave me dry.

I will not give what you refuse to return.

Take what I have given,

but know this,

there is nothing left for you here.

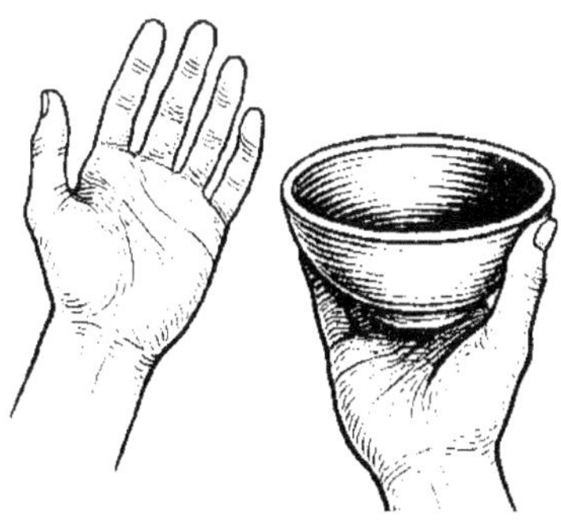

Section II – The Pulse of Want

Overwhelmed

I am not burning the candle at both ends.
I have dropped it into an inferno,
watched it disappear into the roar,
watched wax become nothing
but smoke curling toward an exit
I cannot reach.
The weight of everything is a flood,
but I am not drowning,
I am the flood.
I spill over the edges,
rushing through cracks I never sealed,
overflowing into hands that only demand
more, more, more.
And when there is nothing left to give,
I siphon from myself.
Drink from my own plasma,
wring blood from my veins,
carve time from my bones

just to fill the mouths of expectation.
My body clenches around this pressure,
teeth grinding into dust,
jaw locked so tight I wonder
if I could shatter it with a single thought.
My heart rattles against my ribs,
a caged animal thrashing,
fighting to break free or shut down,
I can't tell which.
I feel my pulse in my throat,
a frantic, choking rhythm
as if my own body
is trying to swallow me whole.
I am a hair trigger,
held down by a brick,
pressed beneath a weight
that doesn't ease,
doesn't let go,
just fires and fires and fires again,
until I forget where the recoil ends

and I begin.

I balance on a knife's edge,

toes curled over the line

between endurance and collapse.

My muscles scream, rigid, coiled,

tight as a noose pulled slow,

a tension that never snaps,

never releases,

just pulls and pulls and pulls

until I feel my skin thinning,

stretched to the point of tearing,

a heartbeat away from unraveling.

Old habits call to me,

like shadows whispering my name

in the hush of an empty room.

They come in familiar forms,

wrapped in silver and sharp edges,

stitched into the seams of my skin.

A blade tracing the map of my failures,

each scar a place I have already been.

Section II – The Pulse of Want

The pills hum in their amber cages,
rattling like an offer,
like a way out,
like an ending wrapped in the softness
of no more.
And then there is the bottle,
the one constant,
the only thing that never leaves,
never hesitates,
never asks me to be more
than I have the strength to be.
It does not need me to smile,
does not require me to exist
in any form other than broken.
It waits, always within reach,
an open door to oblivion.
I am so goddamn tired.
Not the kind that sleep can fix,
not the kind that coffee can burn away.
I am tired in my cells,

tired in the marrow of me,

tired of carrying this weight

when I can barely carry myself.

I close my eyes,

not to rest,

but to pretend,

just for a second,

that I do not exist.

And for a second,

it feels like relief.

For a second,

it almost feels like peace.

Section II – The Pulse of Want

A Body That Won't Listen

I love you so selflessly,

I have become selfish.

What else is there to do with a love like this,

one that has carved its purpose into my ribs,

stitched itself into the fibers of my being

until I am nothing but a vessel for wanting you?

I was made to love you.

To keep you warm when the world was cruel.

To hold your happiness like something sacred,

like a glass heart I was never meant to drop.

And now,

what am I,

if not that?

A can opener with no more cans.

A gas station in a world where no one stops.

Something that once had use,

and now only rusts.

I see people grasping at life,

fingers desperate around the edges of their days,
pleading for just one more hour,
just one more breath,
just one more chance to stay.
And yet,
without you,
I don't want to be here.
The air inside me burns,
oxygen eating away at me
like rust swallowing iron.
My heart thuds against my ribs,
pumping something thick and wrong,
acid through my veins,
dissolving every reason to keep moving forward.
And my brain,
God, my brain,
it is a broken machine,
endlessly whirring,
endlessly replaying,
thinking only of what I beg it to forget.

Section II – The Pulse of Want

I keep living,

even against my wishes.

Even against my will.

Even though every part of me knows

I was never meant to live without you.

Section II – The Pulse of Want

IV Drips and Empty Promises

Life is breath and blood,

bones bending to the weight of days,

the slow erosion of flesh

against the sharp edges of time.

It is movement,

unstoppable, indifferent,

a train with no brakes

barreling toward an end

we all pretend isn't waiting.

But love,

love is the sickness.

It starts as a warmth in the chest,

a fever mistaken for light.

A pulse quickens,

veins dilate,

something inside blooms and spreads,

sinking its roots into the marrow

where it cannot be cut out.

Section II – The Pulse of Want

You call it beautiful.

You call it fate.

But I have seen the bodies it leaves behind.

The slow decay of certainty.

The atrophy of trust.

The skin pulling tight over ribs

like a house abandoned,

a structure collapsing

under the weight of ghosts.

Love does not kill you quickly.

No, it lingers,

suffocating, starving,

deteriorating the quality of what remains.

A paralysis of the soul.

A slow, rotting death

that comes with a smile,

a whispered promise,

a touch that feels like home

until it turns into a wound

that never heals.

Section II – The Pulse of Want

I have seen the symptoms:
the sleepless nights,
the hollow chest,
the way hope curls in the gut
like a tumor refusing to die.
I have watched the infected
drag themselves through years
begging for just one more dose,
one more hit
of something that was killing them
from the start.
There is only one cure.
A release.
A letting go.
An unhooking of the IV,
a final breath drawn without a name on the lips.
A quiet surrender to the inevitable.
Call it mercy.
Call it peace.
Call it euthanasia.

But know this,

I will not die gasping for something

that was never meant to keep me alive.

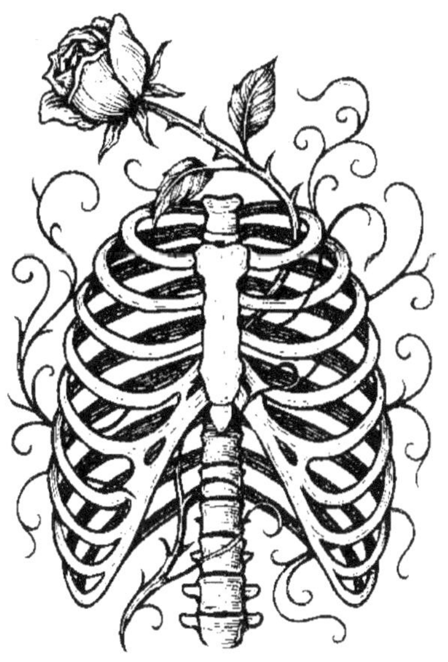

Section II – The Pulse of Want

Love, the Terminal Disease

Life is motion, breath, the quiet hum of existence.

A body that endures, even when it shouldn't.

Even when it aches beneath the weight of its own ruin.

Life is the cruel joke—

survival for the sake of survival,

no matter how hollow, no matter how broken.

But love,

love is the sickness.

It begins as something warm, something vital.

A pulse skipping beneath skin,

the rush of oxygen that fools you into thinking

you are more alive than you were the moment before.

It is not sudden, not violent, not merciful.

It is a slow unraveling.

It weaves itself into your bones,

makes a home beneath your ribs,

until you can no longer tell where you end

and the disease begins.

I wanted it.

God, I wanted it.

Wanted to be consumed, to drown in it,

to know the kind of fever

that makes you believe in something bigger than yourself.

I wanted her.

And she was the worst kind of cure.

The kind that only deepens the wound,

that keeps you just alive enough to suffer.

She gave me doses too small to heal

but too potent to ignore.

A touch that soothed the symptom but never the cause.

A love that filled my hands but never my chest.

And still, I would have taken it.

Would have let it burn me clean,

let it take the marrow, the lungs,

every last soft part of me,

if it meant feeling it fully.

If it meant her.

But love,

love does not let you go easy.

It leaves you gasping, wanting,

stretching your hands toward something

that has already walked away.

So I choose the only kindness left.

A stillness.

A silence.

A final breath,

her name on my lips,

one last longing exhaled into the dark.

Not because I do not want to live—

but because I cannot live without.

Section III Bound by Desire

"The body speaks in tongues the mouth is too shy to utter."

This is where restraint unravels. These poems descend into the sacred tension between power and vulnerability, the fierce tenderness of surrender, and the language spoken only in skin and breath. Desire is no longer hinted at, it is embraced, explored, and exalted. There is no fear in these lines, only the fearless intimacy of being seen and touched completely. These pieces are love stripped of metaphor, written in the language of fingertips, lips, and pulse.

Section III Bound by Desire

You Were Never Meant To Be Untouched

Come closer.

I want to feel the hesitation in your breath,

the weight of your pulse as it flutters beneath my hands.

You are silk wrapped in quiet rebellion,

soft where you should be,

unyielding where you shouldn't.

And yet,

you give.

I feel it in the way your body lingers between command and surrender,

in the way your breath stammers when I pull you closer,

when my fingers tangle in your hair,

tilt your head just so,

until I can see the quiet ache in your throat,

the way it waits for my touch,

the way it asks without asking.

Do you know what you do to me?

Section III Bound by Desire

Do you feel the gravity between us,
this slow, inevitable pull?
Like the tide, like the sky bending to the horizon,
like something ancient and inescapable.
You lean into it,
into the heat, into the weight of my hands
as they find their way,
as they map you with purpose,
as they remind you,
you were never meant to be untouched.
Your breath is a whisper against my skin,
your body an answer I haven't yet asked for,
but will.
Oh, I will.
There is no rush.
Only this moment,
this slow, excruciating unraveling,
where I take my time,
where I press my lips just close enough
for you to wonder if they will ever touch.

Section III Bound by Desire

Where I hold you still,

one hand wrapped around your throat,

not to take, not to break,

but to remind you,

you are mine.

And you,

you wouldn't want it any other way.

Section III Bound by Desire

Where Petals Become Flames

Tell me.

No, whisper it.

Let it spill from your lips like honey, slow and thick,

coating the air between us,

a confession, a surrender.

You already know how I take my claim,

fingertips pressing into your skin like ink on parchment,

leaving love marks, bruises that bloom like midnight violets.

Proof that you are mine in the way the moon belongs to the tides,

in the way your breath hitches when I speak your name low,

commanding, certain.

I don't ask for flowers.

I don't need them.

You are already something soft that opens for me,

a petal caught in the heat of my palm,

a storm waiting to be unraveled beneath me.

Flowers and sex,

they are one and the same when it's you,

sweet, delicate, waiting to be devoured.

Your body all over me,

and yet, not close enough.

Never close enough.

Like wildfire and gasoline,

like silk and steel,

like need and surrender,

we are both the match and the flame.

So tell me again.

Say it so there's no air left between us.

So that every syllable lingers, tattooed on your tongue.

Tell me all the ways you're mine.

And I'll remind you just how much I love to hear it.

Section III Bound by Desire

Surrender is Spelled With My Name

Say my name,

Say it.

Let it linger, let it slip from your tongue

like a whispered sin,

like something forbidden but far too good to resist.

Love letters drip from my lips

as I pull you close,

as my fingers trace the hesitation in your breath,

as I find the fragile pulse at your throat,

press just enough for you to feel it,

to remind you that surrender is not weakness,

it is a choice.

And you,

you choose this.

Lick sensual syllables between parted lips,

let them spill in that trembling voice,

that quiet plea wrapped in velvet,

in heat, in need.

Section III Bound by Desire

Your body is a language I have studied well,

every arch, every gasp,

every way your skin betrays you

before your mouth ever dares to speak.

Tongue tied in bold type,

you cannot find the words,

but I do not need them.

Not when I can hear them in your breath,

in the way your body moves against mine,

in the way you tremble when I take my time,

slow, deliberate, unrelenting.

You are waiting for permission to fall.

I give it to you,

with my hands in your hair,

with my teeth at your throat,

with the weight of my body pressing you into this moment

until nothing exists outside of it.

Taste our unrestrained fate,

feel it burn against your skin,

let it sink into your bones,

until you forget where you end and I begin.

Say my name.

Say it like it belongs to you.

Because tonight,

you belong to me.

Section III Bound by Desire

Indulge

"Indulge me," you whisper,

a request, a demand, a promise,

woven between the heat of your breath

and the tremor in your pulse.

I watch you hesitate,

caught in that perfect space between defiance and need.

You don't move—yet.

Waiting for permission, waiting for the inevitable.

You've always been good at this game,

pressing against the edges of control

just enough to feel them tighten around you.

Just enough to see if I'll let you get away with it.

I won't.

"Watch your mouth," I warn,

low, quiet,

but you hear the command beneath the softness,

feel it like an unspoken thread pulling you in.

Section III Bound by Desire

My fingers brush your lips,

a featherlight tease before my thumb lingers at the edge,

a silent dare, an unspoken test.

You part them, reckless, wanting,

but you know better than to speak.

Not until I allow it.

There's a flicker in your gaze,

that last spark of resistance before the fall.

And then, you give it to me.

All of it.

Your breath stutters as I claim what's mine,

the curve of your throat beneath my palm,

the soft gasp that betrays your patience,

your body shifting, melting, surrendering.

"Claim what's yours," you taunt,

as if I hadn't already begun,

as if I hadn't spent every moment

mapping you with my hands,

memorizing the way you yield

and the precise second you unravel.
So I take more.
The arch of your back against my chest,
the slow, deliberate slide of my fingers
tracing the pulse at your wrist,
your heartbeat telling me everything
your lips refuse to say.
I could make you wait forever.
But not tonight.
Tonight, I take you to the edge,
slow, patient, cruel,
until you forget how to resist,
until the only word left on your tongue is my name.
"One last kiss," you plead,
but we both know better.
There is no such thing as last
when it comes to us.
Only the next.
And the next.
And the next.

Section III Bound by Desire

Because I don't let you go

until I decide I'm done.

And I am never done.

Section III Bound by Desire

Bound by Lust

What would happen if we kissed?
Would the world tilt,
or would it stop altogether,
holding its breath
as I press my lips to yours,
as I pull you deeper,
as I make you forget how to stand on your own?
You're already swaying,
caught between hesitation and hunger,
between restraint and the inevitable.
Your breath comes uneven,
shallow, desperate,
as if the air itself is thick with longing,
as if your body knows
what your lips have yet to confess.
Lick my delicious fiction.
Taste the story I have written into your skin,
one slow stroke at a time.

Section III Bound by Desire

I trace paragraphs down your spine,
punctuate each gasp with my teeth,
write sonnets into the hollow of your throat,
press poetry between your thighs.
Every shudder is a stanza.
Every moan, a metaphor.
Every broken whisper of my name,
a masterpiece.
Can I get a witness?
Does the night hear how you come apart for me,
how your body sings before you find your voice?
Would the stars shudder with you,
watching the way I take you in pieces,
only to put you back together
one trembling breath at a time?
We are bound by lust,
by the way my hands pin you beneath me,
by the sound you make when I tell you to stay still,
by the way your body betrays you,
offering, yielding, aching,

before I have even asked.

You press against me,

silent pleas written in the way your body moves,

in the way you arch,

in the way your pulse stutters under my touch.

I see the surrender in your eyes,

the war already lost,

the battle never truly fought.

You have always belonged to this moment.

I slide my hand to your throat,

not to silence you,

but to feel the sound of my name

vibrating against my palm,

a trembling hymn, a whispered confession,

a prayer you didn't know you were saying.

Your pulse is frantic,

your body wrecked with longing.

I drag my lips down your skin,

slow, reverent,

until you are trembling beneath me,

until I have pulled every last thread of hesitation from you,

until all that's left is need.

What would happen if we kissed?

You already know.

But you will beg for it first.

Section III Bound by Desire

When Your Body Melted Into Mine

Come here

Slow.

Let me watch the way your breath shifts

when you step into my gravity,

the way your body hums

before I even touch you.

I stoke the flames with a whisper,

the edge of my voice curling against your skin,

and already, you shudder,

like you've been waiting for this,

like you've been starving for it.

I want to leave the lights on,

watch the moment you let go,

see the heat rise beneath your skin,

watch the need spill over

in gasps and parted lips,

in the way you grasp at me,

as if touch alone could quench

what I've set ablaze.

When lightning strikes twice,

it is not chance.

It is intention.

It is the weight of my hands guiding you,

commanding you,

pulling you apart

only to piece you back together

in pleasure too deep for words.

You are humming with electricity,

charged with need,

a storm of want

caught between your lips,

in the soft, breathless pleas

that I will answer

with no hesitation.

And when the fire consumes you,

when every nerve sings,

when your body melts into mine,

shaking, spent,

but deeply satisfied,

I will hold you in the afterglow,

trace the embers on your skin,

and watch you smile,

because you were always meant

to burn for me.

Section III Bound by Desire

The Right to Remain Breathless

I watch you,

trapped between want and surrender,

your breath caught like contraband kisses

between parted lips.

You know I see it.

That pulse at your throat,

the way your body betrays you

before you even speak.

I step closer.

You don't move.

I like that.

Fingers trace the line of your jaw,

a slow, deliberate claim.

You shiver,

but it's not fear, is it?

Waive the right to remain silent.

I want to hear you.

Every gasp, every broken whisper

as I take what's mine,

as I teach you how it feels

to be kept under lock and key.

No bars, no chains,

just my body against yours,

the heat of my palm at your throat,

not to silence,

but to remind you

who holds the key.

I tilt your chin up.

Eye contact.

Always.

There's nowhere to run,

no need to hide.

You don't want to be free, do you?

Not when freedom

is this,

the slow slide of my fingers down your spine,

the grip that lingers just enough

to leave a mark,

a quiet brand of ownership

you'll feel tomorrow,

when I'm not here,

when you crave more.

Good behaviour won't save you.

Not tonight.

Not when I know what you need.

Not when I can feel it

in the way your body gives,

in the way your breath stutters

before I even touch you.

This is no prison.

It's something else entirely.

Set me free, you whisper,

but your hands pull me closer,

nails dragging across skin

like a signature,

like a plea you don't mean.

And I,

I press my lips to your ear,

smirk against your skin,

and remind you,

darling,

You were never free to begin with.

Section III Bound by Desire

When Restrain Becomes Worship

I watch you,

the way your body hums in the hush of waiting,

breath caught between restraint and release,

fingertips curling at the edges of anticipation.

Your eyes,

those blue grey eyes, wild and wide,

shining with something between defiance and surrender,

like a storm that begs to be calmed,

but only by my hands.

I take my time.

Devouring you from a distance,

tracing possession through the air between us.

My gaze, slow, deliberate,

fingers your skin before I do,

a whisper of heat you feel everywhere.

Do you like this?

The tension?

Section III Bound by Desire

The way I make you wait,
how I hold your need in my palm and press it,
just enough to make you ache?
Come here.
Intertwine the intangible,
let me lace my hunger through your breath,
draw you into me until restraint is nothing but a ghost
moaning between our mouths.
Your lips,
French kissed in cursive,
soft vowels and bitten consonants,
a language rewritten between gasps,
spilled down my throat with each eager pull.
And still,
I do not touch.
Not yet.
I let the silence thicken,
weighted with command,
watch the way your body betrays you,
shifting, pressing, needing.

Section III Bound by Desire

Patience, sweetheart.

Let me hear it,

that trembling sigh, the one just for me,

that breathless whisper of surrender.

Sans-serif sighs and whispered lullabies,

notes sung against my skin,

soft, pleading, waiting to be taken.

And when I do,

when my hands finally claim what's already mine,

when my teeth scrape over pulse points,

when your knees threaten to fail beneath the weight
of this wanting—

You'll understand.

This was never about the touch.

It was about the space between.

The waiting.

The wanting.

The moment you gave in,

before I even laid a hand on you.

And now, I will.

Section IV – Wilted Skin, Withered Self

"Some parts of me are gardens. Others are graveyards."

This section walks the path of self-discovery through decay. These poems speak of identity fractured by abandonment, confidence eroded by cruelty, and the slow fading of one's reflection under the weight of being unseen. But even here, in the withering, there is beauty. These verses aren't about giving up. They are about acknowledging the parts of ourselves we bury to survive, and the quiet hope that something might still grow in the soil of our ruin.

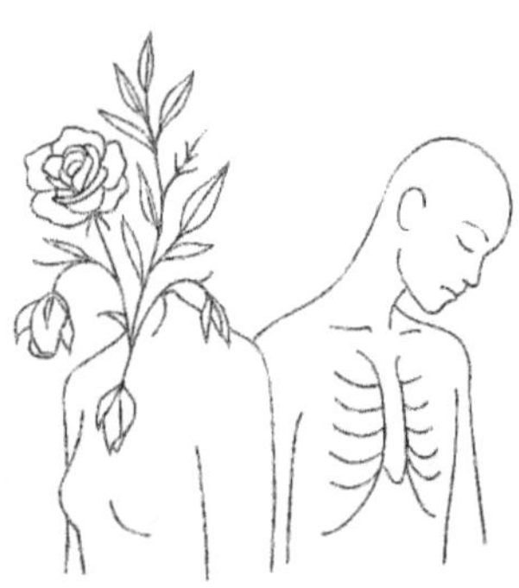

Section IV – Wilted Skin, Withered Self

I Was Ready to Die Until I Realized I'd Have to Forget Her

The spined tendrils stretched, webbed in darkness,

a lattice of something more than knowing,

less than flesh.

Their voices were not voices,

but something deeper,

a pulling, a question braided into marrow:

Are you ready?

And I nodded,

because I have always lived in surrender,

because I have never feared the edge,

except in this moment,

when I knew what I could not leave behind.

Her.

Her name was the iron in my blood,

the gravity that held me

when the universe unraveled into spectral light.

Her absence was a wound,

a star collapsing inward,

a scream with no sound.

I reached for her with hands that were not hands,

with want that was not just want,

but the last remaining reason

I have ever been human.

And I saw it,

the kaleidoscope ache of longing,

tears fracturing light into the colors of her laughter,

the warmth of her skin pressed into the spaces

I thought could never be filled.

I could have let go,

could have become something else,

spun into the vast and endless quiet.

But love,

love is the only truth I have ever known,

and she is the only thing that makes dying

unthinkable.

Section IV – Wilted Skin, Withered Self

Where My Hands End and You Begin

I do not hold you,
I house you.
You are not a presence,
not a visitor to my body,
but the marrow inside my bones,
the ache in my ribs when I breathe too deeply,
the weight in my stomach that I do not resent.
I carry you without trying,
without effort,
without question.
Your name is written in the lining of my lungs,
so that every exhale is a whisper of you,
so that every inhale is a longing for more.
And I do,
I long.
I long in ways that cannot be softened,
cannot be reasoned with,
cannot be undone.

Section IV – Wilted Skin, Withered Self

My hands were made for your skin,

a truth I did not know until the first time I touched you,

until the first time my fingers learned the shape of your name.

And now,

Now, they ache.

They ache in the hollow spaces where your hands should be,

in the emptiness between fingers that once knew how to thread into yours,

that once folded into the divinity of your palms like prayer.

I have never believed in God,

but I have believed in you,

and maybe that is the same thing.

Because you,

you are written into the blueprint of my existence,

woven into the fibers of my body like veins beneath skin,

etched into the quietest corners of my mind,

where even I cannot erase you.

Section IV – Wilted Skin, Withered Self

I do not know how to exist without you.

I do not know how to stop loving you.

You are the pulse in my fingertips,

the shiver on my spine,

the hum beneath my ribs,

the static in my chest when I see you,

when I don't see you.

Because the absence of you is not silence,

it is a frequency too low for human ears,

but my body hears it.

My body feels it.

It is a soundless ringing inside my bones,

a static hum inside my heart,

a weight, a pull, a knowing,

That I will never be whole again

without you.

Section IV – Wilted Skin, Withered Self

Epiphany v1 – AKA I Am The Love That Doesn't Wait to Be Chosen

I once thought love was something you held,
a thing delicate enough to be cupped in trembling hands,
a fire to be fed, a river to be crossed,
a bridge between two hearts that could,
in time,
collapse beneath the weight of the world.

But then I saw it,
not as a thing outside myself,
not as a gift given or taken,
but as the marrow in my bones,
as the breath between my ribs.

I am not a man who loves you,
I am love for you.

It is not an action I take,
not a choice I weigh in the quiet hours,
not a tether I could sever and walk away from,
it is the fabric of me.
It is the skin I wear,
the voice in my throat,
the map my blood runs through.

It is the moment before sleep,
when your name is the last syllable my mind cradles,

the first thought that stirs as morning breaks,
the sunlight warming the place where you should be.

I am love for you in the way roots are earthbound,
the way rivers do not decide their course,
the way the moon does not try to pull the tide,
it simply does.
It simply is.

I do not love you the way a poet writes,
carefully curating each phrase,
each metaphor, each breath,
I love you the way wind moves through trees,
without hesitation,
without needing permission,
without ever considering another way to be.

I am love for you in the way the sea is salt,
the way fire is heat,
the way the sky, no matter how clouded,
has always been blue beneath.

And if you ask me,
what happens if you never come back?
If you choose another path,
if your hands never reach for mine again,
if my name fades from the edges of your lips?

Still,
I am love for you.

Not as a man waiting in the rain,
not as a shadow standing at the edge of your world,
not as a ghost haunting the spaces we shared.
But as something greater,
something weightless and certain,
something unbreakable and eternal.

I am love for you the way the earth turns,
even when no one is watching,
even when the night stretches long,
even when no one speaks its name.

And that,
that is the epiphany.

I do not hold this love.
I do not carry it like a burden.
I am it.
And whether you ever come home to it or not,
I will always be.

Section IV – Wilted Skin, Withered Self

The Axis I Spin Upon

I once thought love was a thing of hands,
of pulse-quickened touch,
of lips parting like the hush before dawn.
I thought it could be carried, like water in cupped palms,
that it could spill, evaporate, be lost to the thirst of time.

But now, I see,
love is not a thing I hold.
Love is the tide in my veins,
the hymn in my marrow,
the wind that moves through me, unseen but known.

I do not love you like a man pressing petals in a book,
preserving something fragile, afraid of its fading,
I love you as the wildflowers love the rain,
as the sky kneels to touch the horizon at dusk,
as the stars burn knowing they will never touch the earth.

I am not a keeper of love for you.
I am love for you.

It is written in the hollows of my ribs,
stitched into the curve of my breath.
It is the rhythm my heart beats to,
the silver thread woven through my soul's tapestry,

the gravity tethering my spirit to yours,
unchosen, unshaken, undeniable.

I love you like the ocean craves the moon,
like the river aches for the sea,
like autumn surrenders to winter's hush,
not in fleeting moments,
not in words left trembling on my tongue,
but in the quiet knowing of things that are.

If I were to break apart into dust and light,
scatter myself across the corners of this world,
every particle, every whisper of me
would hum your name in the spaces between stars.

You are not just someone I love.
You are the axis my being spins upon.
The echo that lingers in an empty room.
The place where my mind rests when all else is still.

And if you ask me,
what if you do not return?
What if you slip from my world like mist in the morning?
What if your hands never reach for mine again?

Still, I will be.

Still, I am love for you.

Like a fire that warms even those who do not sit beside it.
Like a lighthouse that stands, even for ships that do

not return home.
Like the moon that still rises, even when unseen.

This,
this is the epiphany.

Love is not something I hold for you.
It is not a candle that wavers,
nor a road that ends.
It is the sky beneath which you walk,
the air that sways through your hair,
the quiet, steady hum in the chambers of the universe.

It is not a choice.
Not a burden.
Not a thing that time can erode.

It simply is.
I simply am.
And whether you ever return to it or not—
I will always be

Section IV – Wilted Skin, Withered Self

Epiphany V2 – This Isn't a Love Poem, It's a Constant

You once told me you didn't think this would last,

that the weight of time would wear it thin,

that feelings like this flicker,

brief as a match struck in the wind,

a flare that fades into nothing.

But I am still here.

More certain that I will wake tomorrow

thinking of you

than I am that the sun will rise.

Because the sun is a habit,

but you are a pulse,

a rhythm that does not falter,

a thought that does not ask permission to exist.

I know you have been left before.

I know you have watched backs turn,

doors close,

words meant to stay

slip through cracks like water
you could never hold.
I know you have learned not to trust permanence,
have taught yourself to question
the hands that say they will not let go.
But I am still here.
I have watched the moon disappear
and still believed in the tide.
I have stood beneath empty skies
and still trusted the stars were waiting.
And I know this,
I know that no matter how much time stretches
or how many nights unravel between us,
there is not a single version of tomorrow
where I do not wake with you
pressed into the quiet places of my mind.
You have doubted this.
You have doubted me.
And I cannot blame you for that.
Doubt is the armor we wear

when too many wounds have been carved

by hands that swore they would never harm.

But if you stripped it away,

if you stood with your chest bare

and let the light in,

you would see,

this does not fade.

It does not waver,

does not buckle beneath the weight of distance,

does not shrink when met with silence.

It lingers,

not as a ghost,

but as a fire that refuses to burn out.

And maybe words are not enough,

maybe you need time,

maybe you need proof

written not in ink,

but in the days that pass

where I am still standing here,

still feeling this.

So I will give you time.

I will give you every tomorrow

until you believe in them,

until you stop searching my hands

for an exit wound,

until you look at me

without waiting for me to leave.

And when the years fold into each other,

when time wears its edges smooth,

when the world is quiet

and breath is something borrowed,

my last will not be spent

clutching at memories

or reaching for things I never had.

It will be spent on you.

Because I am more certain

that my dying breath will be used

to say your name

than I am that the stars

are still there tonight.

And that,

that is the only proof I can give you.

But I hope it is enough.

Section IV – Wilted Skin, Withered Self

This is How I See You (And I Never Blink)

I have spent hours studying you,
not just the way light gathers
at the edges of your face,
but the way it surrenders completely
to the depth of your eyes,
a place where entire storms have raged,
where softness still finds its way through.
Your beauty is not just a sum of parts,
though if it were, it would be a masterpiece
rendered by a hand that knew
how to shape something devastating.
The curve of your lips,
sculpted to hold both laughter and silence.
The way your hair falls,
like a thought left unfinished,
deliberate, effortless,
always captivating.
But it is not just that.

Section IV – Wilted Skin, Withered Self

Not just the way your skin

drinks in the warmth of a room,

or the way your cheekbones catch shadows

like whispered confessions.

Not just the way your collarbones

press against the soft fabric of your world,

how your body moves with a grace

that doesn't beg to be noticed,

but still commands attention.

It's the moments between beauty.

The way you laugh in three different shades,

one where your head tilts back,

full-bodied and unguarded,

like a song you don't realize you're singing.

Another, where you pull your chin in slightly,

like you're trying to hold it back but can't.

And then that mischievous little chuckle,

the one that sounds like a secret,

as if you know something the rest of the world doesn't.

Section IV – Wilted Skin, Withered Self

It's the way you pull faces when I look at you,

as if you think you need to distract me,

as if your beauty requires a disclaimer.

You don't see what I see,

that every version of you is breathtaking.

Even the one with a smirk,

even the one with raised brows

and mock-seriousness in your gaze,

even the one that tries to hide.

And God, your voice,

sweet southern warmth with a country twang,

like the way whiskey lingers,

like a song played on the porch

while the world softens at the edges.

You could read anything aloud

and I'd still hang onto every syllable,

because it's you,

woven into sound, into air, into me.

And still, you doubt.

You stand before mirrors

that cannot hold the truth of you,

listening to the echoes of voices

that were never meant to shape you.

But I see you.

Through every guarded smile,

every quiet moment where you wonder

if you are enough.

You are.

You always were.

I wish you could step into my gaze,

just once,

to see what I see.

To feel the way the world pauses

when you enter a room.

The way your laughter rewrites the air.

The way your sadness lingers in the bones of a place

long after you've gone.

You are unforgettable,

even in the ways you try to disappear.

You have never been just a face,

never just a body.
You are the kindness you give so freely,
the fire you hide beneath your skin,
the way your love for your children
is stitched into everything you do.
You are the strength in softness,
the depth in quiet moments,
the presence that lingers long after you've left.
I have spent hours studying you,
and still, I have barely scratched the surface.
There is too much of you for one lifetime,
too much light, too much depth,
too much of everything that makes me
utterly, hopelessly yours.
And I will spend a lifetime more,
learning every version of you,
loving you through every season,
until you understand,
you have never been anything
but extraordinary.

Section IV – Wilted Skin, Withered Self

The Moment the Universe Made Sense

You sat before me, spine curved inward,
as if folding yourself into something smaller,
something easier to bear, something less visible.
Your hands twisted in your lap, knuckles pale,
as if they could hold together the pieces of you
that felt too broken to touch.
You said you felt pathetic.
The word fell from your lips like a stone,
sinking into the space between us,
heavy with every unspoken ache,
every quiet war you had fought alone.
But I saw you.
Not the way the world does,
not as skin and breath and fleeting moments,
but as something eternal, something luminous.
Like the night sky had broken itself
into constellations just to carve your shape into existence.

I lifted my gaze to yours,

held it there, unwavering,

as if I could tether you back to yourself.

And when I told you that you were beautiful,

not despite this moment, but because of it,

I felt the universe exhale around us.

For the briefest second,

I watched the sadness in your eyes hesitate,

as if it had forgotten how to exist in the presence of love.

And then,

like the slow bloom of dawn against an endless horizon,

you smiled.

It was not a grand thing,

not a wide, sweeping gesture of joy.

It was the ghost of something softer,

a fleeting imprint of light against the shadows.

But it was enough.

In that moment, I knew.

Knew it the way the tide knows the pull of the moon,
the way roots know how to find the earth.
My purpose was not to save you,
you were never something that needed saving.
My purpose was to be the mirror
that always reflected your beauty back to you,
even when you could not see it for yourself.
And I swear to you now,
with the weight of the stars as my witness,
that for as long as breath lingers in my lungs,
for as long as the world turns beneath our feet,
I will spend my days making sure
you never forget the way
you made the universe feel small
in the presence of your existence.

Section IV – Wilted Skin, Withered Self

Where the Blade Can't Reach

I could carve you out of me,
take a blade to my chest and excavate the feeling,
dig deep, past ribs and sinew,
past marrow and memory,
past every nerve that thrums your name.
And still,
you would remain.
You are not something I carry,
not a weight I could drop,
not a thing to be shed like skin in summer.
You are the shadow I cast
in light and in dark,
the echo that lingers long after sound has died,
the scent of rain that stays in the air
long after the storm has gone.
I cannot be without you.
Because being without you
is not being at all.

Section IV – Wilted Skin, Withered Self

You are woven into me,

stitched beneath my skin,

threaded into my veins like roots in soil,

tangled in me like ivy on stone,

and I do not want to be untangled.

I am built from this feeling,

constructed from this need,

designed to want you,

to reach for you,

to ache for you,

whether you are near or distant,

whether you are silent or speaking,

whether you know it or not.

I do not love you in moments.

I do not want you in waves.

There is no ebb.

No flow.

Only this.

Only always.

Only you

Stream of Consciousness (Written After the Poems)

This wasn't written in the clarity of healing.
This book, like the others before it, was written in the ache,
the kind that seeps into the walls of your life and repaints everything in grief.
Most of these poems came from nights I wouldn't wish on anyone.
Nights spent staring at the same ceiling,
heart pounding for someone who wasn't coming back,
lungs dragging breath through liquor and nitrous and pills,
through scars I carved just to make sure I could still feel.

I didn't write to be read.
I wrote to survive.
To bleed something that wasn't blood.
To scream without waking the neighbors.
To bury a love I couldn't bury in any other way.

I lost her.
Or maybe I lost myself in loving her.
Maybe both.
Because when she stepped away,
everything else started stepping too,
my sense of worth, my grip on the world, my desire to wake up.

Stream of Consciousness

And yet,
somehow, I made it through.
Not because I was strong,
but because I was stubborn enough to keep writing.
Because even when my body was giving up,
my hands still found the page.

The poems in this book are that version of me:
unwashed, trembling, high, hungover, raw.
They are desperate and lonely and unforgiving.
They are not the man I am now.
But they are how I got here.

Because something changed.
She came back.

Not in some perfect, cinematic way.
Not with fanfare.
But real. Quiet. Soft.
The kind of return that feels like a sunrise you didn't
realize you'd survived the night for.

She told me she loved me.
She said she always had.
Said she was scared, because if it went wrong, it
wouldn't just break her;
it would ruin her.
She said she didn't want to lose me.
And now she doesn't have to.

She wrote "I love you" in her handwriting.
I tattooed it to my leg.

Stream of Consciousness

Because I never want to forget that even the most
broken chapters
can lead to the kind of love that holds you when
you're whole and when you're not.

She has seen me at my worst.
Held space for the ghost of who I used to be.
And still, she stays.

So if this book feels like a farewell to something, it is.
It's a goodbye to the grief that raised me.
A memorial to the pain that taught me how to write.
And a thank you to the muse who walked through all
of it
just to meet me here,
on the other side.

Never give up…..

Edgar J. Wilde

Section V – Descent & Revelation

"Even the fall teaches us something about the weight of wings."

These poems live in the in-between, between collapse and clarity, between breaking and becoming. They do not shy away from the stumble; instead, they document it like scripture. Addiction, escapism, and emotional unmooring wind through these pieces, but so does self-awareness. Sometimes we must fall to see what we're made of. And even when it feels like we are dissolving, there is something sacred in seeing ourselves clearly in the descent.

Section V – Descent & Revelation

They Were Never Trees – They Were Warnings

I step forward, the air thick with whispering roots,
twisting beneath me like veins of something ancient,
something waiting.
The trees loom, their bodies bent, heavy with silence,
their faces carved from time,
gnarled mouths twisted in unreadable expressions.
I do not know them, but they know me.
A thousand eyes, hollow yet piercing,
drip with the weight of what they've seen.
Their gaze coils around my ribs,
tightens.
I cannot breathe without feeling their judgment,
or is it recognition?
The path ahead is nothing but a suggestion,
a trick of light through tangled limbs.
I press on,
but their murmurs are not carried by wind,
they are stitched into the marrow of my bones,

reaching backward, pulling forward,

reminding me.

And then, I see them.

Not strangers. Not ghosts.

Not something watching, but something waiting.

Their eyes, my eyes.

Their mouths, my silence.

Their cracked bark, my breaking.

I am not lost in this place,

I am home in it.

I reach out, fingers brushing the rough surface of myself,

and the trees exhale,

the weight of my own becoming settling into the roots.

Section V – Descent & Revelation

Even Bungle Looked Away When Zippy Couldn't Save Me (Mushroom Trip)

The laughter bubbled and frothed,

spilling out of my mouth like an overfilled glass of soda,

fizzing, sparking, popping against the roof of my mouth,

rolling over my tongue in a flavor that wasn't quite laughter,

but something sweeter,

something warmer,

something older.

It didn't stop at my mouth.

It trembled down my throat,

rattled across the xylophone of my ribs,

Playing unknown notes

In an unrequested order

spilling out, cascading echoes,

each breath pushing a new wave of uncontrollable delight.

Section V – Descent & Revelation

The peekaboo trees outside leaned in.

I caught them.

They froze,

awkward, unnatural,

twisted mid-motion like guilty children caught sneaking past bedtime.

I blinked.

They resumed their play.

The window latch watched me.

It wasn't just a latch anymore.

It had a presence.

The iguana's unblinking eye,

glass smooth, slick with some unnamed intelligence,

glancing sideways, matter of factly, as if I had finally noticed it.

The bush by the fence waved.

Not by the wind.

Not by force.

But by choice.

Satisfied to finally be seen.

Section V – Descent & Revelation

And the porch light,

that faithful yellow glow,

winked at me.

Not as an invitation,

not as a warning,

but as acknowledgment.

As if it knew.

As if it had been waiting.

I inhaled. Drawing smoke into my lungs like Lewis
Carrol's caterpillar.

The world rushed in,

eager, desperate, pressing into the space around me,

the air dense with something I could almost touch.

I exhaled. Smoke rings drifting to nothing.

It pulled away,

retreating, reluctant,

as if I had pushed it aside.

I breathed the world toward me.

I breathed it back.

And I laughed.

Section V – Descent & Revelation

A laugh that did not belong to me.

A laugh that did not sound like my own.

A laugh that twisted in the air,

spiraling, stretching,

warping into something not entirely human.

And then,

Something else laughed too.

It arrived like an afterthought,

like a breath of cold air in a warm room,

like a second shadow where one was already enough.

Not sudden.

Not violent.

Just present.

The touch was not sharp.

It was not claws or hooks.

It was familiar fingers,

curling around my wrists,

tracing up my arms,

sliding over my ribs like a mother's hand smoothing crumpled bedsheets.

Section V – Descent & Revelation

"Come home."

Not a demand.

Not a plea.

Just a statement of fact.

I was one of them.

One of the dark.

One of the mold.

One of the rot.

Something tugged at my ankles,

light, barely there,

like the memory of a grip rather than a real one.

It was patient.

It had waited this long.

It could wait longer.

The music,

Ah but the music,

the music did not allow it.

It crashed into the dark like a tidal wave of light,

rolling, pulsing, spiraling outward,

bathing me in colors that did not exist.

Section V – Descent & Revelation

I saw the sound.

The bassline rolled like molten gold,

thick, syrupy,

dragging through the air like honey spilling from a broken jar.

The guitar trembled in jagged slashes of blue,

ribbons of electric cyan,

snapping, cracking like the bite of a whip.

The voice curled out in tentacles of violet,

tender and longing,

a spectral hand tracing the length of my spine.

Every note shifted shape,

a prism turning in an unseen light,

colors never staying the same,

bleeding, folding, twisting.

I was inside the song.

I was the song.

I was nothing but color,

weightless, untethered,

a flicker of light in a universe of sound.

Section V – Descent & Revelation

Colors only seen on deep sea creatures

Existing where light shouldn't.

Jellyfish motions with extraterrestrial hues

Everything loved me.

But they had never left.

They had only waited.

At the edges of the light,

just beyond the reach of the music,

watching,

coiling,

hungry.

The moment the notes began to fade,

they returned.

A shadow curling at the base of my spine,

a whisper against my ribs,

a hand sliding over my throat,

not choking,

not clawing,

just reminding me it was still there.

"You cannot hide in the color forever."

Section V – Descent & Revelation

The glow dimmed.

The music dulled.

And in the silence,

they grew bolder.

Sliding between the colors,

spilling through the cracks,

writhing like oil through water,

a presence with no shape,

a voice with no sound,

a weight with no form,

But real.

And then,

A tendril brushed my lips.

Not cruel.

Not violent.

Intimate.

As if it wanted to know,

to see,

if I would still let it in.

If I would still say yes.

Section V – Descent & Revelation

My breath hitched.

My body froze.

And in that instant, I knew,

if I let it,

if I welcomed it,

if I stayed too long in this moment,

I would never leave again.

I grabbed at something,

anything.

Something safe.

Something familiar.

Something that had no sharp edges,

no crawling shadows,

no creeping sense of unease.

Children's TV.

The old ones.

The pink, long-eyelashed hippo,

soft, smiling, androgynous.

George.

What even was it?

Section V – Descent & Revelation

Zippy.

A puppet with no clear species,

a giant unhinging mouth,

a voice that grated,

what the fuck was Zippy supposed to be?

And Bungle.

A bear?

A man in a bear suit?

Something that wasn't quite either?

The more I thought about it,

the less sense it made.

And for a moment, it was funny.

But the dark had been waiting.

And it did not care for nostalgia.

It had only ever let me wander.

Let me play.

Let me breathe, just enough to forget it was still there.

But now,

Now it claimed me.

The grip was firmer this time,

fingers turning to vines,

vines turning to ropes,

ropes turning to roots,

burrowing into my skin,

weaving into my ribs,

tethering me down, down, down.

I clawed against them,

felt them flex,

tighten,

pulse like living muscle.

Like they had been waiting for me to be ripe enough to take.

"Come home."

Not an invitation.

Not a suggestion.

A sentence.

A verdict.

The world tilted.

The colors of the music bled black.

The laughter was gone.

Section V – Descent & Revelation

The vines yanked,

And I fell.

The dream had followed me.

For as long as I could remember.

In a life of impermanence,

it had been the one ever-present thing.

It had always chased me.

But tonight,

I chose to fight.

I chose to chase.

I chose to see.

The hallway stretched before me.

Endless.

A corridor of memory,

lined with doors,

some half-open,

some cracked just enough to see inside,

some waiting, silent, patient, untouched for decades.

I walked.

Slow.

Section V – Descent & Revelation

My steps did not echo.

The air here was too thick for sound to travel.

It swallowed every movement,

smothered every breath.

I stopped at the first door.

It swung open,

A glimpse of a younger me,

Hiding.

Inside duvet covers.

Knees tucked to my chest.

Breath held tight,

the cotton warmth of the fabric pressing in,

a child's illusion of safety.

I took another step.

The next door cracked wider.

Hiding.

In the woodland behind the house,

kneeling in the damp earth,

pressed low beneath the twisting branches,

the leaves whispering against my skin,

the wind muffling the sound of footsteps on gravel.

Another door.

Hiding.

Inside a closet,

pressed between hanging clothes,

dust in my nose,

stale breath in my throat,

the gap in the door just wide enough to see the darkened room beyond.

Why was I always hiding?

One more door.

8 years old. Staggering. Plied with alcohol and coins. Unpleasant birthday scenes.

The last door at the end of the hallway stood open.

Waiting.

I stepped inside.

The drawers pulled in behind me.

Splintered wood at my back.

The air stagnant,

thick with the scent of carpet,

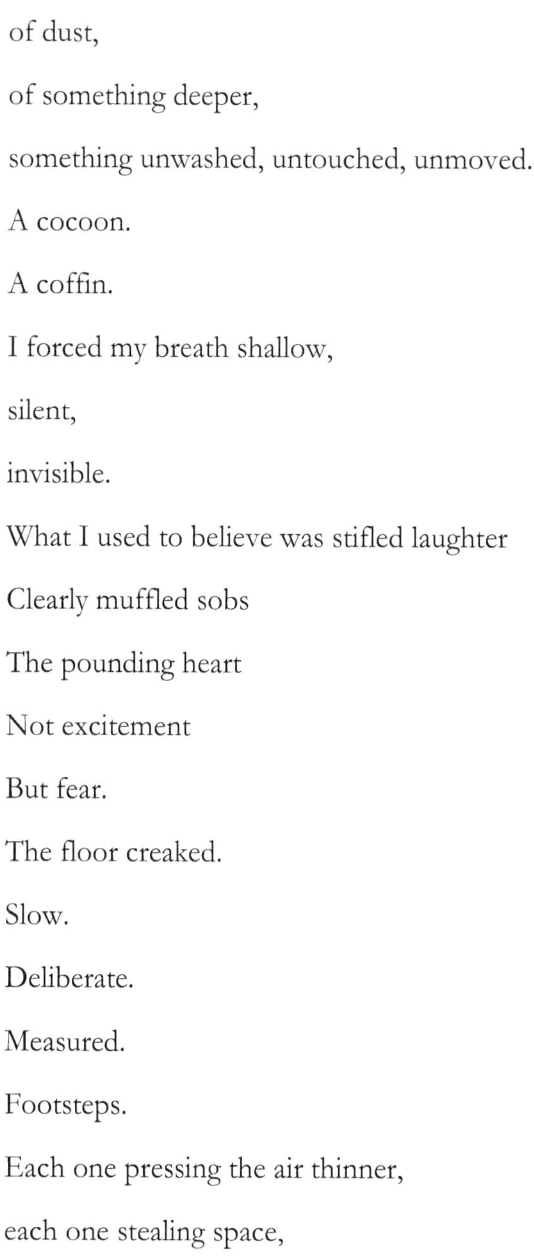

of dust,

of something deeper,

something unwashed, untouched, unmoved.

A cocoon.

A coffin.

I forced my breath shallow,

silent,

invisible.

What I used to believe was stifled laughter

Clearly muffled sobs

The pounding heart

Not excitement

But fear.

The floor creaked.

Slow.

Deliberate.

Measured.

Footsteps.

Each one pressing the air thinner,

each one stealing space,

shrinking my world,

narrowing it to this one tiny space beneath the bed.

The shadows on the walls shifted.

A shape moved in the dark.

The unseen monster.

The drawers groaned as they were pulled free.

One by one.

The slats of wood scraped.

The space grew smaller.

Its breath,

Heavy.

Thick.

The smell filled my lungs,

wrapped around my throat,

The air pressed in.

I closed my eyes.

A silent scream from above,

The stick insect,

eight feet long,

perched on the ceiling,

motionless but screaming,

its neck flared like the creature from Jurassic Park,

its mouth open, stretched, frozen in a sound I could not hear.

The weight of fear filled my chest,

spread into my limbs,

settled into my bones.

I had nowhere left to go.

Nowhere left to hide.

And then,

Her hand.

Warm.

Soft.

Steady.

Fingers curled around mine,

gentle, unshaking, effortless in their certainty,

like she had always been there,

like she had always meant to be there.

I turned my head,

And there she was.

Section V – Descent & Revelation

[Her Name].

Even in this induced state

She came to me

In thoughts

In dreams

Sitting beside me,

silent, waiting, knowing,

eyes that held no questions,

no demands,

no pressure,

just acceptance.

The kind of acceptance that doesn't need to be spoken aloud.

The kind of acceptance that just is.

She did not ask why I was here.

She did not ask why my hands were shaking.

She did not ask what I had seen.

She did not need to.

She already knew.

Her presence was enough.

The warmth of her skin in my palm,

the slow, quiet inhale and exhale of her breath beside me,

the soft press of her thigh against mine where we sat together,

the steadiness of her,

the realness of her,

Perfectly imperfect,

the weight of her reality,

In my unreal haze

The safe space

My subconscious turned to

Knowing the only thought

Which would protect me,

Was her.

All of it was enough.

Enough to drown out the shadows.

Enough to quiet the footsteps.

Enough to erase the stale air beneath the bed.

Enough to remind me that I was still here.

Section V – Descent & Revelation

That the past was just a story.

That the monsters could not touch me anymore.

That I was not alone.

That I had never truly been alone at all.

That for the first time,

in a life spent hiding,

in a life spent small,

in a life spent holding my breath,

I was not afraid.

I was not numb.

I was not lost.

For the first time,

I was safe.

And I held on.

Realizing now,

For certain

These feelings for her

Are real.

Unchanging.

Forever within me.

Section V – Descent & Revelation

She Is What the Moon Remembers

She moves like the hush of silver light,
spilling through the wounded clouds,
a quiet insistence against the weight of shadow.
The sky, bruised and weary,
tries to keep its secrets,
but she—she has never been one to be hidden.
She is the color that refuses to drown,
the ember caught in the throat of the wind,
the quiet pulse of violet and indigo
where the storm once stood.
Even when the night folds itself into silence,
even when the sun turns its face away,
she remains,
not waiting, not fading, but burning.
The moon knows this.
Knows that she is not a reflection,
but an echo of something greater,
a light born from an unseen fire,
a radiance that does not beg to be noticed

but cannot be ignored.

She is the breath of the horizon,

the ink spilled into the sky,

the moment the darkness forgets itself.

Even in the absence of day,

even when the world swears itself to shadow,

she is the brilliance that remains,

unshaken, untamed, eternal.

Section V – Descent & Revelation

Before the Mirror Knows Her Name

There is a moment,

before the mirror wakes,

before the world remembers its rules,

when she exists

exactly as the universe made her.

No artifice.

No gloss.

Just the wild, gentle aftermath

of sleep's embrace still clinging

to her skin.

Her hair,

a constellation of tangles and chaos,

like galaxies caught mid-spin.

Strands reach

in every unplanned direction,

and I swear

I have never seen

a more honest kind of beauty.

Section V – Descent & Revelation

Her face, unpainted,
is not undone—
it is unveiled.
The shadows beneath her eyes
are not tiredness,
but poetry.
Proof she dreams in full color
and wakes still holding pieces
of those distant places
between her lashes.
She doesn't know
how much I love her like this,
when the world hasn't yet touched her,
when the only glow on her cheeks
comes from the ghost of sleep
and not the sun.
She stretches,
half-conscious,
murmurs a name that might be mine,
and I feel like God

must have paused

when crafting her collarbones.

There is nothing missing.

There never was.

Not in this soft, sacred disarray,

not in the honesty

of a yawn still half-formed,

not in the lull

that lives in her eyes

before they open fully.

This is the hour

the stars envy.

This is the frame

no artist could replicate.

This is her

before she becomes

the version she thinks

she must be,

and it is the version

I would choose

a thousand lifetimes over.

Section V – Descent & Revelation

Where Heat Teaches Us to Stay

The water knows no names,
only the soft gravity of bodies
lowering into warmth.
Steam lifts like a hush
between our shoulders,
a fog of quiet reverence.
Here, skin is not just skin,
it is parchment softened by heat,
and every droplet writes a vow
we never had to speak.
Your back finds my chest,
and the world becomes smaller,
a ripple shrinking into the shape of us.
My arms fold around you,
not to hold,
but to surrender.
To cradle the ache we've carried
and soak it loose.

Section V – Descent & Revelation

The bath does not rush.

It waits,

like we do,

for the stillness beneath the surface

to speak in silence.

Your breath slows against mine,

and I learn again

that love isn't fireworks,

but the gentle erosion

of everything that isn't needed.

Fingers trace the waterline of your thigh,

not a touch,

but a pilgrimage.

And your hair, wet and unbound,

becomes a river I could drown in

willingly,

joyfully.

There is no need

for language here.

Only the shifting of knees,

the murmur of skin,
and the sense
that even the bathwater blushes
to witness such quiet devotion.
We are not washing away,
we are steeping,
saturating,
becoming.
Two shapes in a single warmth,
disappearing
into each other.

Section V – Descent & Revelation

The Siren's Pour

It starts as a whisper,
low, sweet, threaded with honey,
a song curling through my ribs,
soft enough to pretend I don't hear it.
I have made a home in drowning,
worn the undertow like a second skin,
learned to drift when the pull gets strong,
to let the tide carry me deeper.
The bottle sings,
a siren with lips of amber,
hips smooth as glass,
eyes dark and endless as the sea.
She does not beg.
She does not plead.
She does not have to.
She only opens her arms,
tilts her head,
and I am already stepping forward,

salt on my tongue,

longing in my throat.

I tell myself I could stop.

If I wanted to.

If I needed to.

But I don't need to.

Not tonight.

Not yet.

She hums when I let her in,

settles warm in my chest,

presses her lips to my temple

and tells me I am safe,

tells me the storm is over,

tells me I do not have to fight tonight.

And I believe her.

But the cost,

oh, the cost.

My body, a wreckage of mornings after.

My hands, trembling like broken compass needles.

My pulse, slowed thick by consequence.

Section V – Descent & Revelation

I have paid in blackouts and bruises,
in apologies I don't remember making,
in nights that unravel into nothing.
And still, she sings.
Still, the tide pulls,
the bottle waits,
and my hands are already reaching.
But control should not feel like drowning.
And maybe, just maybe,
there is something waiting beyond the waves,
something lighter,
something cleaner,
something that does not demand my body
as a sacrifice for silence.
Maybe.
But tonight, the siren sings,
and the tide is rising,
and I am still learning how to swim.

Section VI – The Strength in Her

"She does not shout to be heard. Her silence has its own gravity."

This final section is a reclamation. After all the ache and undoing, we arrive here, not untouched by the storms, but still standing. These poems celebrate quiet strength, quiet resilience, and the softness that survives even the worst weather. They honor not only the strength of those we love, but the strength we carry, often unnoticed, within ourselves. It is not a triumphant ending, but a grounded one: steady, present, and full of quiet power.

Section VI – The Strength in Her

She Carries The Sky Like It's Nothing

the steady ground beneath unsteady steps,

the hands that catch, the voice that calms,

the one who carries without complaint.

But even mountains feel the weight of sky,

even rivers ache beneath the moon's pull.

And you, with all your strength,

are allowed to feel the weight you carry.

You are not a mess.

You are not a burden.

You are not something to be fixed or lessened.

You are a storm that bends the trees

but never breaks them.

You are fire that warms, not destroys.

You are a lighthouse standing tall,

even when the waves try to swallow you whole.

So let me be the ground beneath your feet.

Let me hold the sky for a while.

You need no one to keep you standing,

but if you stumble, I will be here.

Not to catch you, but to remind you

that you have always known how to rise.

And I see you.

In all the ways you give, in all the ways you endure.

You are strength woven in human form.

And I have never been prouder

to know someone

who carries the world,

and still finds a way

to let in the light.

Section VI – The Strength in Her

Built From Storms and Still Blooming

There is a strength in you

that does not shout to be seen.

It does not beg for recognition

or demand the world take notice.

It is quiet, unshaken—

the kind that holds others steady,

even when the ground beneath you shifts.

But strength is not the absence of struggle.

It is not the refusal to bend.

Even the tallest trees bow in the wind,

even the sun sets before it rises again.

And you,

you have weathered storms

that would have broken lesser souls.

You have carried the weight of others

without ever asking who would carry you.

So let me.

Not because you are weak,

but because even the strong deserve rest.

Even the light deserves a place to soften.

You are not a burden,

you are not a mess,

you are the wildflower pushing through cracks,

choosing to bloom despite it all.

And I,

I am honored to stand beside you.

To witness the way you rise,

to see beauty not in spite of your battles,

but because of them.

You are a wonder.

A force.

A story written in resilience,

and I will always be proud

to know you,

to support you,

to remind you that even the strongest

are worthy of love,

of rest,

of being held.

Section VI – The Strength in Her

Gathering Hours Like Wildflowers

You do not arrive gently,
you are born of fire.
The kind that lingers long after it's passed,
the kind that warms a house
through a bitter winter,
even if the house forgets
who lit the match.
I have watched you carry
more than your hands were made to hold.
You gather broken hours
like wildflowers no one else saw,
and you braid them into
something your children can call
a childhood.
You are the kind of mother
who holds galaxies together
with a voice soft enough
to soothe a storm,

but fierce enough

to make the sky pause

before raining on your daughter's laugh.

You love like a promise

made in a life before this one,

quiet, relentless,

and somehow still gentle.

The world has tried

to fold you into smaller shapes,

to tell you that strength

is volume,

that beauty is silence,

that devotion

means never asking for more.

But I have seen you,

not just when you smiled,

but when you didn't.

When you thought no one was watching,

when you were tired

but kept going anyway,

when you stood still

so others could lean.

And I need you to know:

None of it went unseen.

You are not soft because you're fragile,

you are soft because you are sure.

Because you know that real power

never needs to shout.

It simply stays.

And heals.

And rises.

You are not a chapter

in someone else's story.

You are the spine.

The pulse.

The author,

the ink,

and the reason the page matters at all.

So if you ever find yourself

shrinking to fit inside a version of love

that cannot hold all you are,

remember this:

A woman like you

does not beg to be kept.

She does not barter

her worth for comfort.

She knows.

She knows

that the person meant for her

will never be afraid

of her flame.

They will come closer,

not to tame it,

but to warm their hands

and thank the stars

that it chose to burn for them.

Section VI – The Strength in Her

Lunch for Two in the Warehouse Parking Lot

We sat in the soft hum of the parked car,
the windows fogged gently with quiet,
the kind of silence that doesn't need filling.
She brought the leftover pizza,
I brought the drinks,
and between us,
something small became something whole.
The box opened like a shared secret,
the crust slightly curled,
cheese congealed just enough to prove
this wasn't planned,
but still perfect.
I handed her a slice like an offering,
fingertips brushing in that unspoken way,
the way people say I'm here
without needing to say it.
The toppings had slid a little in the journey,
mushrooms crowded one side,
a single olive clung to the crust

like it didn't want to let go.

And I thought,

maybe love is like that,

not symmetrical,

not always neat,

just two people

picking pieces from the same mess

and calling it a meal.

We didn't talk much.

Didn't need to.

There was warmth in the way she leaned back,

eyes closed for just a second too long

after that first bite.

I watched her from the edge of my straw,

thinking how rare it is

to be full on so little,

how sometimes,

half a pizza and a shared afternoon

can taste more like forever

than candlelight ever could.

A Note by (Her Name)

Edgar - If you have followed my Instagram account you will know that my poetry is dedicated to and about a woman I have only referred to as (Her Name) (although KDP does not like the use of square brackets hence the switch up here), out of respect for her privacy. We have been apart since August of 2024, and in that time I have loved her everyday and longed for us to find our way back to each other. The waiting paid off and now [Her Name] and I are together. We have had a relationship that has been unique, ups and downs but always present for each other when needed and hour long conversations pretty much daily. Finally, the universe aligned in a way that brought us back together and now we are happy, healing, and planning for our marriage.

Below are some words from [Her Name] herself, Miss Ashley…..

I am not a poet, I am not one with words. So the ones that follow can be nothing more or less than from my heart.

To ~~Edgar~~ Mark,

you are and have always been my thread, you are my world, who I cannot be without; I am bound to you and I love you.

Yours, Always,

Ashley (Her Name]

Also by the Author

Closing Note

To those who have walked with me through these pages from:

Roots of Rot and Ruin,
through Seeds of Shadow and Soil,
past Petals of Poison and Pain and
Thorns of Tragedy and Truth,
and now to The Wilting of Winter and Worry
 - thank you.

You have followed me through the darkest forests of longing, through the tremble of unspoken love, the ache of almosts, the wreckage of waiting. You have witnessed a soul unraveling and reaching, searching and holding on, even when there was nothing but memory to hold.

Each book has been a map, etched in blood, in ink, in breath, leading not only toward her, but also back to myself. This final installment is a farewell to the ache that raised me.

A goodbye to the ghosts I once called home.

These poems were born in the hollow spaces between us, back when we were just two orbiting souls, drawn to each other, yet never quite meeting in the light. But in the words of (Her Name) there was always a thread, thin and trembling, stretched between our hearts, the kind that doesn't break, no matter how far it's pulled.

And now, after months of poems and pain, of hope and hesitation...
she is no longer a wish I whisper into the dark.
She is beside me, growing, healing, laughing, living, and choosing this life with me, every day.

So, this is not an ending, but a turning.
From ache to anchor.
From longing to love.
From dreaming of a future,
to building one together.

If there are books to come, they will speak not from the wounds of the past, but from the warmth of what we've built.
The love that endured.
The strength we found in each other.
The peace that came not from forgetting, but from finally arriving.

Thank you, truly, for holding space for these words, and for me.
You've witnessed the ache.
Now, maybe one day, you'll witness the joy too.

As my muse and I move forward into the new chapter of our lives, with plans for marriage and our future growing together, I am thankful for this outlet and the supportive community of poets and artists that have encouraged me to keep on writing my feelings, which kept me from falling off the edge and making some decisions that cannot be undone, which would have stolen the happiness I am now experiencing with my muse, (Her Name)……. Ashley.

With all my heart,
— Edgar

Also by the Author

Poetry

The Withering Collection

- Roots of Rot and Ruin (Kindle Bestseller)
- Seeds of Shadow and Soil (Kindle Bestseller)
- Petals of Poison and Pain
- Thorns of Tragedy and Truth
- Wilting of Winter and Worry

Fiction

- Keepsake (Short Stories)

www.ingramcontent.com/pod-product-compliance
Lightning Source LLC
LaVergne TN
LVHW010657110826
845149LV00014B/3137
* 9 7 9 8 9 9 2 1 9 3 1 5 2 *